Retold by Donna Alexander
Illustrated by Ray Goudey

www.steck-vaughn.com

Characters

Narrator 1	a young boy
Narrator 2	a young girl
Geppiggo	the woodcarver
Pignocchio	a piggy bank
Princess Sue	a kind fairy princess
Wart Hog	the bad pig
Mr. Pigfeld	the famous director

Scenes

Scene 1	Geppiggo's Workshop
Scene 2	Pignocchio's Schoolroom
Scene 3	New Pork City Stage
Scene 4	Geppiggo's Workshop

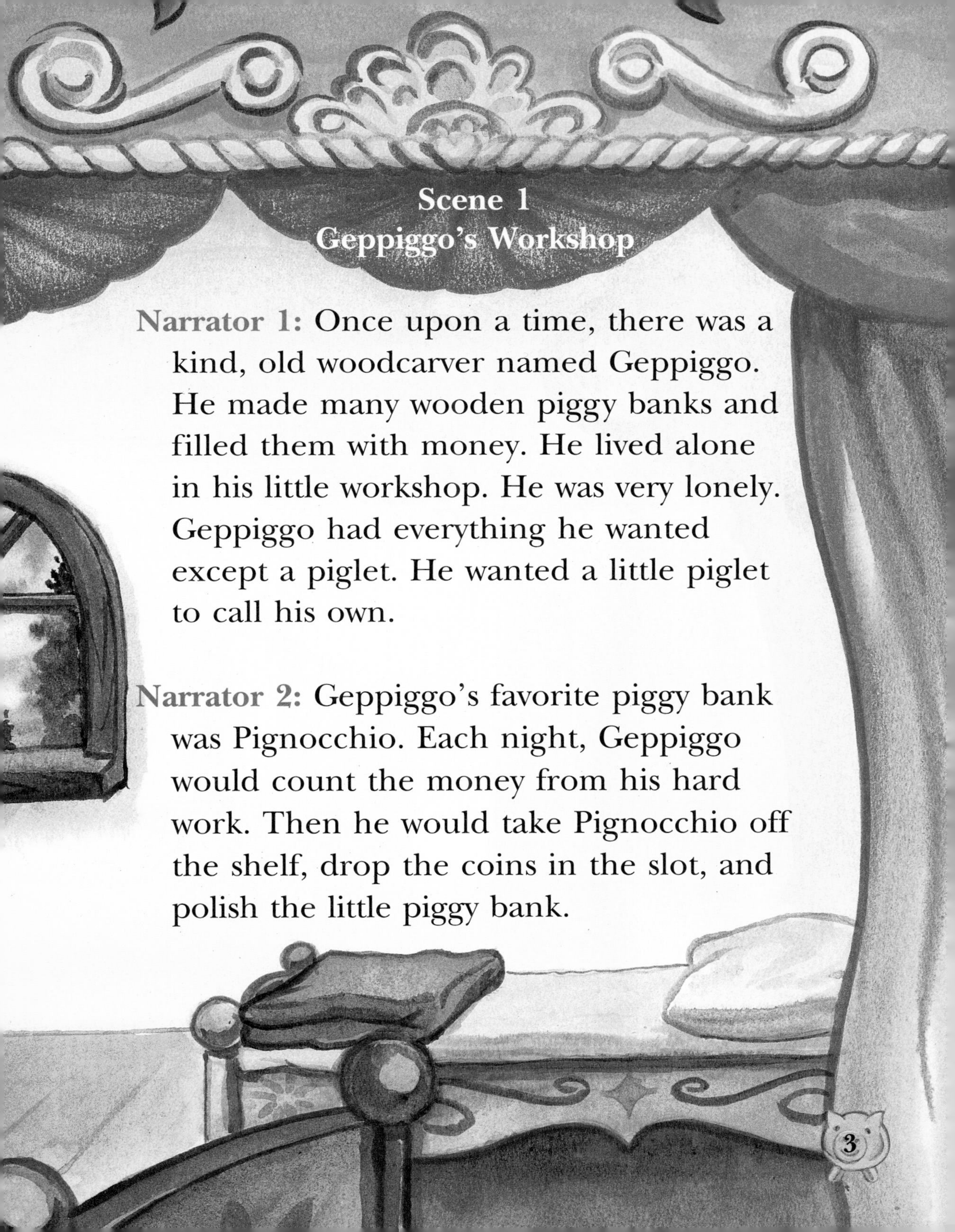

Scene 1
Geppiggo's Workshop

Narrator 1: Once upon a time, there was a kind, old woodcarver named Geppiggo. He made many wooden piggy banks and filled them with money. He lived alone in his little workshop. He was very lonely. Geppiggo had everything he wanted except a piglet. He wanted a little piglet to call his own.

Narrator 2: Geppiggo's favorite piggy bank was Pignocchio. Each night, Geppiggo would count the money from his hard work. Then he would take Pignocchio off the shelf, drop the coins in the slot, and polish the little piggy bank.

Geppiggo: *(polishing Pignocchio)* Well, Pignocchio, here's the money I made today. I sure wish you were real. Then you could be my son.

Princess Sue: *(watching from the window)* Poor old Geppiggo. He wants a real pig so much. Maybe I can help. I'll wait here until he goes to sleep.

Geppiggo: *(yawning)* It has been a long day. I think I'll go to bed now. Good night, Pignocchio.

(Geppiggo lies down and goes to sleep.)

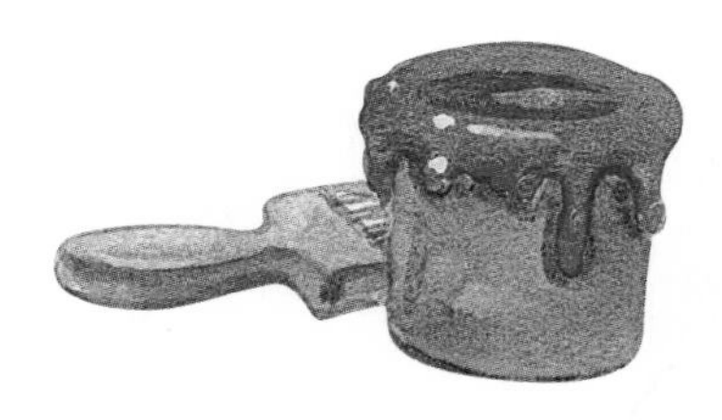

(Princess Sue tiptoes into the room. She takes Pignocchio from the shelf.)

Princess Sue: *(waving her wand)*

Little Piggy, made of wood,
Come alive and talk.
Geppiggo wants a little pig,
So I will make you walk.
If you show that you are good,
And never tell a lie,
I'll come back and change you then
From wooden to real life.

(Princess Sue holds out her cape. Behind the cape, switch the piggy bank for Pignocchio. Then Princess Sue exits.)

Pignocchio: Look! I can move my legs! I can walk! Oink, oink, wheeeeee!

Geppiggo: *(sitting up, rubbing his eyes)* What is all this noise? Pignocchio, look at you. You can walk! How did this happen to you?

Pignocchio: Princess Sue was here. She did this. I am still wooden, but someday I will be real. She told me to be good and never tell a lie.

Geppiggo: Oh, Pignocchio, I'm so happy! I will teach you how to be good. I will even take you to school. There you can learn to read and sing.

Scene 2
Pignocchio's Schoolroom

Narrator 1: Pignocchio was a good little pig for a long time. Every day, he did his chores and helped Geppiggo in the workshop. He even started going to school and learning how to read.

Narrator 2: Best of all, Pignocchio was singing in the school choir. That is where he met his new friend, Wart Hog. But Wart Hog was not a good pig. He had a plan for Pignocchio. One day, after choir practice was over, Wart Hog shared his plan with Pignocchio.

Aa Bb Cc Dd Ee Ff G

Wart Hog: Pignocchio, you have a great singing voice. You should go to New Pork City and become famous. If you can make it there, you'll make it anywhere. Let's go together.

Pignocchio: Oh no, Wart Hog. I must first run home to ask Papa about this.

Wart Hog: No, no, no! We do not have time. Listen, you'll earn a lot of money for your Papa. That will make him happy. Besides, you want to be a good pig, don't you? ***(Pignocchio nods his head.)*** Then you MUST sing for everyone. That's what a good pig would do!

Pignocchio: I want to be a good pig. And I'd like to earn money for Papa. Okay, I'll go to New Pork City. But how will we get there? We have no money.

Wart Hog: Silly Pignocchio, aren't you a piggy bank? We will shake the money out of you and buy bus tickets.

Pignocchio: We can't use that money! That is Papa Geppiggo's money, not mine. I could not take it.

Wart Hog: *(crossing his fingers behind his back)* We won't take it, we'll just borrow it. Soon we'll be rich. Then you can pay Papa back every cent.

(Wart Hog shakes Pignocchio. They pick up the coins and exit.)

Scene 3
New Pork City Stage

Narrator 1: When Wart Hog and Pignocchio got to New Pork City, they rented a hotel room. It cost every cent they had left. As Pignocchio lay down to sleep, he began to cry. He was hungry and afraid.

Narrator 2: The next day, Pignocchio and Wart Hog went to a theater. The stage director, Mr. Pigfeld, clapped his hands and cheered when Pignocchio sang.

Mr. Pigfeld: I'll make you a star. Your papa must sign your contract right away.

Pignocchio: *(looks nervous)* I'm sorry, Mr. Pigfeld, but I have no papa. Wart Hog is my agent. Can he sign for me?

Wart Hog: *(bragging)* Sure, I'm the agent.

Mr. Pigfeld: All right then. Sign here. I'll see you tonight.

(Wart Hog signs a paper. All three exit.)

Narrator 1: When Pignocchio told the lie, his snout grew a bit longer. But no one noticed, except the little pig himself.

Narrator 2: That night, Pignocchio sang very well. The crowd clapped and cheered. They even threw money!

Pignocchio:

How much is that piggy in the
toy store?
The one with the small, curly tail?
How much is that piggy in the
toy store?
I sure hope that piggy's for sale.

Wart Hog: Pignocchio, you're great! Look! Even Princess Sue is here.

Princess Sue: *(walking in from the side)* Hello, Pignocchio. Have you been good? Have you remembered that you must never tell a lie?

Pignocchio: Oh, yes. I have been good. I have never told a lie. Oh, oh, oh!

(He grabs his nose and runs off stage. The others follow him.)

Narrator 1: Pignocchio ran off stage because his snout was growing. The next night, Pignocchio sang again, but he didn't sing very well.

Narrator 2: No, he didn't sound good at all. Every time he took in a breath of air, he made a snorting sound.

Pignocchio: *(holding snout, snorting)* How much is that piggy in the toy store?

Mr. Pigfeld: Pignocchio, the crowd is clapping, but some people are laughing. You must sing better!

Pignocchio: I'm trying, but I can't sing without snorting.

Wart Hog: Look, Pignocchio. Princess Sue came to hear you again tonight.

Princess Sue: *(walking in from the side)* Hello, Pignocchio. Have you been good? Have you remembered that you must never tell a lie?

Pignocchio: Oh, yes. I have been good. I have never told a lie … *(shouting)* Oh, no! No! *(grabs snout, runs off stage)*

Wart Hog: *(running after him)* Pignocchio! Wait! What's wrong with your snout? You have to sing, not snort!

(Princess Sue and Mr. Pigfeld shake their heads and exit.)

Narrator 1: The next night, Pignocchio was terrible!

Narrator 2: Yes, REALLY terrible! He could barely get out a note because his snout was so long!

(Pignocchio and Wart Hog enter. Both are holding up Pignocchio's long snout.)

Pignocchio: *(snorts)* How much is … *(snorts, then says)* Oh, no! I can't sing!

Mr. Pigfeld: *(enters yelling)* No singing, no job! You're fired!

Wart Hog: Pignocchio, now look what you have done! We have no money. This is all your fault.

Princess Sue: *(entering)* Pignocchio, have you been good? Have you remembered that you must never tell a lie?

Pignocchio: *(crying)* No, Princess Sue. I have been bad. I ran away from Papa. I spent all his money. I told Mr. Pigfeld a lie. Then I lied to you, too. Now I'll never get to be real.

Princess Sue: *(sweetly)* Now, now, let's get you home. Geppiggo has been very worried. We must think of him now. I'll wave my wand and make your snout small again.

(Princess Sue waves her wand as all exit.)

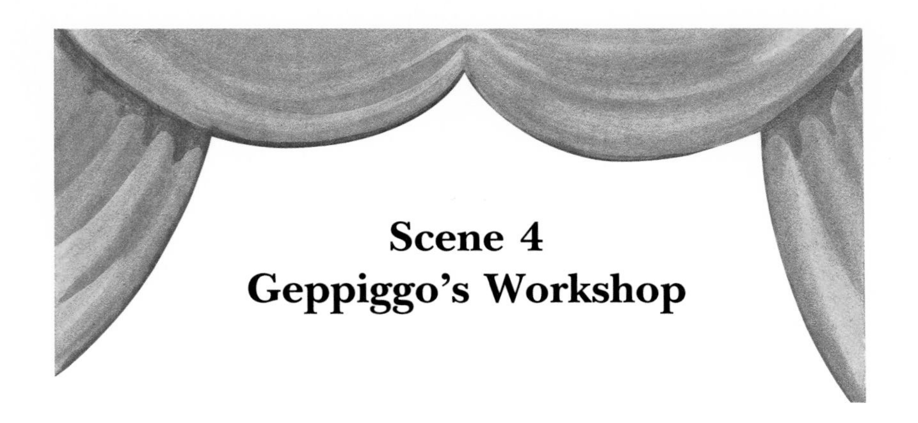

Scene 4
Geppiggo's Workshop

Geppiggo: *(sadly)* Where, oh where has my little pig gone? Where, oh where can he be?

Pignocchio: *(with a broken heart)* Here I am, Papa. I'm sorry that I ran away.

Geppiggo: *(happily)* My son, my son! I'm so glad you came home!

Pignocchio: Papa, please forgive me. I'll never run away again. I spent all your money, but I will pay back every cent.

Princess Sue: *(waving her wand)* Pignocchio, I think you learned your lesson. Now I will make you real.

Pignocchio: Look, Papa! Now I'm real!

Once I was a piggy bank,
Only made of wood.
Then a fairy princess came
And told me to be good.
The way I broke my papa's heart,
How terrible I feel.
The princess waved her wand up high,
So now, at last, I'm real!